SHERLOCK

AND THE
BAKER STREET
CURSE!

SHERLOCK

AND THE
BAKER STREET
CURSE!

SAM HEARN

▀SCHOLASTIC

Scholastic Children's Books
An imprint of Scholastic Ltd
Euston House, 24 Eversholt Street, London, NW1 1DB, UK
Registered office: Westfield Road, Southam, Warwickshire, CV47 0RA
SCHOLASTIC and associated logos are trademarks and/or
registered trademarks of Scholastic Inc.

First published in the UK by Scholastic Ltd, 2018

Text and illustration copyright © Sam Hearn, 2018

The right of Sam Hearn to be identified as the author and illustrator of this work has been
asserted by him.

ISBN 978 1407 16406 9

Printed by CPI Group (UK) Ltd, Croydon, CR0 4YY
Papers used by Scholastic Children's Books are made
from wood grown in sustainable forests.

1 3 5 7 9 10 8 6 4 2

www.scholastic.co.uk

For
Emily
&
Harriet
x

Yearbook

Meet the class ...

SHERLOCK HOLMES
Big brain or big-head? We'll see.

Most likely to ... who knows?
He's such a mystery.

JOHN WATSON
The new kid in school. Loves writing, drawing, eating biscuits and drinking hot chocolate.

Most likely to ... be a doctor –
maybe!

MARTHA HUDSON
A class leader. Funny and super confident.

Most likely to ... succeed at
EVERYTHING!

JAMES MORIARTY

Sherlock's nemesis... He's annoying, selfish and always where you don't want him to be.

Most likely to ... take over the world.

CHARLIE AND SEB

Sneery voiced, evil grinned, trouble-making best pals of James Moriarty.

Most likely to ... cause a stink wherever they go.

DAZ

Loses everything! Yes, everything.

Most likely to ... become a life coach (when he finally sorts himself out).

MR MUSGRAVE
The trusty school caretaker, Baskerville's owner and part of the furniture at Baker Street Academy!

Most likely to ... be pottering around at school after everyone's gone home!

MR BRUNTON
Cool, creative and quirky new teacher at Baker Street Academy

Most likely to ... have an outstanding reputation.

BASKERVILLE
The coolest doggy detective ever! He can sniff out a custard cream a mile off.

Most likely to ... get belly rubs.

London.

Somewhere off Baker Street ... again.

I can't see a thing.

Click

Sherlock?

Sherlock!

Yep. Some things never change.

Sherlock! Where are you?

Over here, John...

Same old Sherlock...

Martha, stop messing about!

I can't see!

Ow! That's my toe!

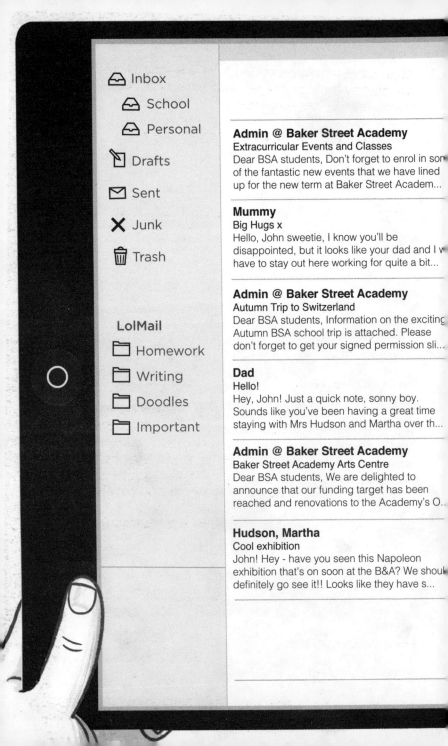

Inbox

School

Personal

Drafts

Sent

Junk

Trash

LolMail

Homework

Writing

Doodles

Important

Admin @ Baker Street Academy
Extracurricular Events and Classes
Dear BSA students, Don't forget to enrol in som
of the fantastic new events that we have lined
up for the new term at Baker Street Academ...

Mummy
Big Hugs x
Hello, John sweetie, I know you'll be
disappointed, but it looks like your dad and I w
have to stay out here working for quite a bit...

Admin @ Baker Street Academy
Autumn Trip to Switzerland
Dear BSA students, Information on the exciting
Autumn BSA school trip is attached. Please
don't forget to get your signed permission sli...

Dad
Hello!
Hey, John! Just a quick note, sonny boy.
Sounds like you've been having a great time
staying with Mrs Hudson and Martha over th...

Admin @ Baker Street Academy
Baker Street Academy Arts Centre
Dear BSA students, We are delighted to
announce that our funding target has been
reached and renovations to the Academy's O...

Hudson, Martha
Cool exhibition
John! Hey - have you seen this Napoleon
exhibition that's on soon at the B&A? We shoul
definitely go see it!! Looks like they have s...

Yeah, it has been great staying here at Martha's house. We start back at school again next week! I can't believe it's come around again so quickly!

OK. Talk to you tomorrow, Mum. Bye for now x

John.

Big Hugs x
Today at 11:30

Hello, John sweetie,

It was very lovely to talk to you earlier – even if I know you're a bit disappointed that we won't be coming home just yet. Your dad and I are really sorry about having to stay on working here for a bit, but I'm sure it won't be for too much longer. I'm so pleased you're having such a lot of fun over there with Martha, Sherlock and Baskerville!

I'll be in touch again as soon as I can. Big, big hugs from me and Dad x x

1

JOHN WATSON

Likes: Reading, writing, doodling.
Wants to be a writer! (maybe a doctor?)

More Adventure... More Trouble... Yeah, yeah,
I know! I'm jumping ahead of myself again. I
just can't help it! Life since I've been at Baker
Street Academy is just *too* exciting. We're
talking crazy with a side of bananas! Add
Sherlock Holmes into the mix and it's a wonder
that my mind hasn't been boggled beyond repair.

Oh, in case we've not met before, I'm John; John
Watson. A student at Baker Street Academy,
currently residing at Mrs Hudson's house, 221B
Baker Street in London with my friends: Sherlock
Holmes, Martha Hudson and Baskerville, the
school caretaker's dog! But I'm getting off-
track again aren't I? Where was I? Oh yeah -
adventure, craziness, bananas and just a little bit
more trouble... Let me catch you up again...

It had been a brilliant summer; Staying at 221B over the holidays with Martha, Sherlock and Baskerville was so much fun!

Mrs Hudson is awesome too - she'd let us take over the front room upstairs (amazing!) and we'd spent the best part of the break using it as our "base of operations" for hanging out and having fun!

But now, school was just a few days away and a cold autumn had started to creep in.

PLUCK!

TWANG!

PLICK!

Mrs Hudson had lit us a fire, Baskerville was stretched out in front of it like a dog-shaped rug and Martha and I were sitting in the big armchairs reading...

Yep. Apart from missing Mum and Dad, this was pretty much as cool as I could imagine things being - and Martha, Sherlock and I had become really good friends :)

PLINK! PLUCK! TWANG! PLICK! SCRAPE! PLUCK!

ARRGH! Sherlock! You're doing my head in! If you're going to stand there twonking away at that thing, you could at least make it sound like a nice tune!

So yeah, like I said - *really* good friends!

3

Sherlock had been staring out of the window for ages, scratching away on an old violin we'd found upstairs in the attic.

He was slowly driving everyone mad - until Martha said she might accidentally push him out of the window if he didn't stop!

I wouldn't mind, but he wasn't even playing a tune... Not that that's unusual around here - Sherlock's got all sorts of odd behaviour traits!

He keeps liquorice pipes in an old slipper

Keeps biscuits in a coal scuttle!

If he wasn't fiddling about on the violin, he'd recently had his head stuck in a pile of old Victorian stories about a detective called Sherinford, and he was talking even funnier than usual!

Anyway, Sherlock put the violin down, went to sit by the fireplace and pulled out one of the disgusting liquorice-flavoured pipe sweets he likes to chew on when his brain is ticking away on some unknown problem.

Just then...

DING DONG!

Exactly right, Baskerville! Now then, my dear Watson. That, if I'm not mistaken, will be Mrs Musgrave. And not before time too!

BOMP! BOMP! BOMP!

And that, by the sounds of it, will be Mrs Hudson showing her upstairs just this very moment!

How would you know who it is? Got X-ray vision now, have you, Sherlock?

Tut tut, Martha! You really must observe a little more.

I saw her coming from the window!

The front room door opened and, just like Sherlock said, in came a slightly flustered-looking Mrs Musgrave.

Splendid!

Mrs Musgrave, please, do come in, won't you?

Ooh, yes thank you.

Sorry for coming round like this in a rush!

I thought I'd come and see if it was OK for you to look after Baskerville a little longer?

While work is going on at school, I mean.

It's just... Mr Musgrave hasn't been himself the last few days, and now he's had, well... He's had a terrible fright...

A terrible fright, you say?!

What seems to be the trouble?

Oh, I'm ever so sorry. It sounds a bit silly now but...

He said he's seen a

GHOST!!

ARTciting news for Baker Street Academy!

Monday 3rd

This straight in from the headteacher, Mrs Cavendish:

Following the announcement over the holidays that we had reached our funding target, I'm delighted to announce that work is nearing completion on the renovations and restorations to the Old Wing of Baker Street Academy. Very excitingly, we'll soon be opening it up as the brand-new Baker Street Academy Arts Wing for students and visitors to enjoy.

We will be making arrangements where necessary to minimize disruption to lessons and the school timetable. In the meantime, I'd like to welcome everybody back to Baker Street Academy.

 0 Comments

A new member of staff for Baker Street Academy:

Baker Street Academy would like to extend a very warm welcome to Mr Brunton who will be joining us as the newest member of staff for this coming term!

Mr Brunton will be stepping into the vacancy left by Ms DeRossi. He comes to BSA from

Hurlstone Academy in Sussex with an outstanding recommendation and we are sure he will bring some creative excitement to his classes! He will also be helping to oversee the schedule of events for the new BSA Arts Wing when it opens later this term, so there's much to look forward to here at Baker Street Academy!

9

BAKER STREET IRREGULARITIES

2

Wow.

That wasn't quite the start back at school that I was expecting... We'd only been there about five minutes and the rumour mill was in full effect! Everybody was already talking about Mr Musgrave and the so-called

BAKER STREET GHOST...

News sure travels fast at *Baker Street Academy!*

"Except it's not exactly news, John," said Sherlock as we strolled through the school corridors. "It's not even accurate!"

"What do you mean?" I asked, a bit confused. "Mr Musgrave did see a ghost, didn't he?"

"Yeah, what do you mean?" echoed Martha suspiciously.

My dear Watson, Martha, there's no such thing as ghosts. And you

know as well as I do exactly what Mrs Musgrave told us—

Yeah we do!

Mrs Musgrave said that Mr Musgrave had had a **TERRIBLE FRIGHT.**

She said he was doing his school checks in the evening, as usual ...

and that he saw a **strange** light ...

somewhere in the Old Wing of the school ...

and what looked like a **ghostly, creepy** figure in the darkness!

And then, when he went inside to see who it was,

they just disappeared!

14

"It does kinda sound like a ghost to me, Sherlock," I agreed with Martha. I felt sorry for Mr Musgrave too; I don't think I'd want to run into anything going bump in the night!

"Well yes, John, it really was a singular account from **MRS MUSGRAVE**, I will give you that.

She is to be congratulated on her clarity of detail. But a **STRANGE** vision in the **DARKNESS** does not a ghost make! It sounds much more like a *'someone'* than a *'something'* if you ask me."

"Well you would say that, smarty pants!" laughed Martha. "And how much longer are you going to keep talking like that Victorian detective, Sherinford? It's getting a bit silly!"

Luckily Martha spotted her friends before Sherlock got too carried away. That's the downside of him being such a brainiac; sometimes he can just be really annoying!

15

I know what you're thinking: as if school needed to be any weirder, right? Just a few months ago we had a teacher who was secretly a *top detective* and our class was caught up in a diamond theft at a museum. Now it looks like we've even got ghosts!

There's no such thing as ghosts.

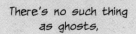

Yeah, yeah, so you said, Sherlock!

Hey, we've got a new teacher.

I know; Mr Brunton, right? I hope he's fun!

And the new Arts Wing sounds like it's going to be cool!

Yep. Despite the first five minutes, it felt good to be back at school. A bit like putting on your favourite pair of comfy slippers! Everybody else seemed to be on top form after a break too...

OOH, LOOK WHO IT IS, EVERYBODY!

Oh, great! Spoke too soon...

Just when it looked like things were all looking good, along came two of Baker Street Academy's resident troublemakers,

SEB MORAN AND CHARLIE MILVERTON.
(EVIL GRINS, SNEERY VOICES AND BEST FRIENDS WITH JAMES MORIARTY.)

IT'S THE THE BAKER STREET ACADEMY SUPERSTAR DETECTIVE: SHERLOCK HOLMES!

AND HIS TWO SPECIAL LITTLE HELPERS. HA HA!

Nice try, Sebastian. Charles. Very original. Is that the best you can come up with while Moriarty isn't around to think for you?

SHUT UP, MARTHA!

YEAH. WE DON'T NEED JAMES AROUND TO THINK OF SOME FUN AND GAMES NOW, DO WE? YOU JUST WAIT AND SEE.

"Ooh, I can't wait!" laughed Martha, as Seb and Charlie slunk off down the hall, scowling.

"Er... What was all that about?" I asked.

"I dunno," said Martha with a big grin on her face. "I'm not about to let those two spoil my day though! Where is James, anyway?"

"He's back in Switzerland for the time being," Sherlock said thoughtfully.

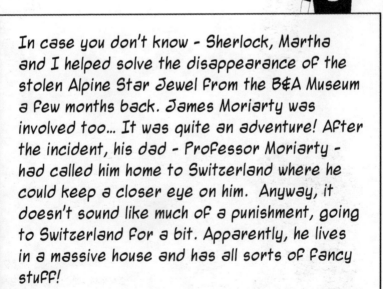

In case you don't know - Sherlock, Martha and I helped solve the disappearance of the stolen Alpine Star Jewel from the B&A Museum a few months back. James Moriarty was involved too... It was quite an adventure! After the incident, his dad - Professor Moriarty - had called him home to Switzerland where he could keep a closer eye on him. Anyway, it doesn't sound like much of a punishment, going to Switzerland for a bit. Apparently, he lives in a massive house and has all sorts of fancy stuff!

So, apart from James Moriarty's two troublemaking friends and, you know, the ghosts and stuff, everything seemed to be pretty much back to normal at Baker Street Academy.

And it turns out our new teacher Mr Brunton is *cool!* Everyone seems to like him. I feel a bit sorry for him having to put up with Charlie and Seb all afternoon though... After our encounter earlier, they were trying extra hard to make a nuisance of themselves in lessons.

(But they did earn themselves detention for the trouble! He he!)

Anyway, Mr Brunton said he's got plenty of "surprises" in store for us, but I thought the best thing was that he's set us a Baker Street Academy-themed writing project to start the term. He said he wants to see what sort of imaginations we've all got. That sounds like the perfect project to me!

I can't wait to get started!

DEAREST SHERLOCK,

HELLO, MY FRIEND! I HOPE YOU'RE WELL?
OH, AND NOT TO FORGET YOUR LOYAL
COMPANIONS, JOHN AND MARTHA TOO, OF
COURSE!

JUST THOUGHT I'D WRITE YOU ALL A
QUICK NOTE WHILST I'M STUCK HERE IN
BORING OLD SWITZERLAND WITH NOTHING
TO DO ALL DAY BUT, YOU KNOW, SKI AND
STUFF. YAWN! I'M SURE YOU'LL ALL BE
SUPER EXCITED TO BE GETTING BACK TO
BAKER STREET ACADEMY FOR ANOTHER
FUN-PACKED TERM - BUT I JUST WANTED
TO LET YOU KNOW THAT EVEN THOUGH I'M
AWAY TEMPORARILY, I HAVEN'T GONE AND
FORGOTTEN ABOUT YOU. NOT AT ALL.

MISSING YOU!

JAMES X

SHERLOCK HOLMES

221B BAKER STREET

LONDON

NW1 6XE

23

Ugh! Moriarty!

Yep. We should've known it was too good to be true.

Sherlock didn't even seem that surprised by the postcard. But Martha? She was not happy ... especially when another turned up in the post first thing the next morning.

OH, DEAR SHERLOCK,

SILLY ME – I FORGOT TO ADD A PS! HOW UTTERLY AWFUL TO HEAR ABOUT POOR MR MUSGRAVE'S UNFORTUNATE GHOSTLY EXPERIENCES. I DO HOPE IT'S NOT A SIGN OF THINGS TO COME! PERISH THE THOUGHT!

YOURS HOPEFULLY,
JAMES M X

SHERLOCK HOLMES

221B BAKER STREET

LONDON

NW1 6XE

He is just so annoying! How did he even know you were staying here?

And how does he know about Mr Musgrave?

"How indeed," said Sherlock.

It's certainly going to make things more interesting.

Then he stuck both postcards on to the fireplace mantlepiece with a big lump of chewing gum. He actually looked quite pleased with himself. I didn't think Mrs Hudson would be though!

After Mrs Musgrave turned up at Martha's house the other night, to tell us about Mr Musgrave seeing a ghost, I didn't think things could really get much stranger - especially when everybody at school started letting their imaginations run wild too...

But boy, was I wrong! Wrong in massive,

GREAT BIG SCARY LETTERS

dripping down the side of a building kind of wrong! I should've expected it, really, the way things were going...

When we got to school that morning there was an ominous warning sprayed all over the side of the Old Wing. It read:

BEWARE THE BAKER STREET GHOST!

C S WOZ
'ERE

BEWARE THE BAKER STREET CURSE!

27

School was totally buzzing!

See, I told you that Baker Street Academy was cursed!

And you didn't believe it!

I don't like it at all. Maybe we can call in some ghost-busters or something?

Ahahahaha! The ghost is gonna get you!

Boo!

Oh, shut up!

Maybe we could ask one of the teachers if we can do a ghost watch after school one night?

That would be amazing!

Now this is definitely creepy! What do you think of that, Sherlock?

Still think Mr Musgrave was imagining things?

Sherlock just smiled and said, "Yes, yes, very creepy, Martha! But like I told you and John before..."

THERE'S NO SUCH THING AS GHOSTS!

"That's not gonna get any more helpful, no matter how many times you say it, Sherlock! Shouldn't we be doing something ... like investigating?!"

"Maybe we should go and have a chat with Mr Musgrave?" I suggested. It couldn't be a bad place to start.

"We could do that indeed, John. And maybe we should, Martha. All in good time! For now, we must observe!"

Typical Sherlock! I wish he'd actually tell us what was going on in that super brain of his!

As far as I was concerned, there was only one thing it could mean: trouble! But by now we were getting pretty used to that around here...

BSA BLOG TEAM CALL

Can you hold a pen, point a camera, tap on a keyboard? Baker Street Academy News needs you! Seen a spooky sight? Had your knees knocked in fright? Felt the chill in your bones? Tell us about it!

Email: news@bsablogteam.com

AFTER-SCHOOL CLUBS:

Survive the spooky season! Look out for details of the after-school workshops all this term. Coming soon!

Autumn School Trip

Outstanding permission slips must be returned as soon as possible to Mrs Staveley.

(FUN WITH)
MR BRUNTON

I think most people found it hard to concentrate at school after the warnings of doom! At least we had lessons to take our mind off things. That afternoon Mr Brunton said,

> As it's such a nice day, it would be a shame to waste it stuck inside.

So we had class outside instead! Cool!

He said it would be good to take our minds off the "ghostly goings-on" at Baker Street Academy and "free up our creative juices" or something. Ha ha!

He took us all round the school grounds looking at the different types of trees. It was a bit weird, but everybody was getting into it - even if Charlie and Seb wouldn't shut up about ghosts and curses. They kept trying to scare everyone until Mr Brunton told them off!

It turned out to be interesting too. You can't really miss the big oak tree at Baker Street Academy, but we also found **ash, birch and chestnut**

and it was cool seeing the old stumps where some had fallen down in a lightning storm. I'm not sure exactly how trees will be useful right now, but no one was complaining!

Well, except for Mr Musgrave... I don't think he was too much of a fan of this new "outside lessons" thing. We heard him getting cross with Mr Brunton when we were looking at trees round by the Old Wing of the school.

BASKERVILLE!

Baker Street Writing Project
Today 15:34

Hello, Baker Street Blog readers!

Brilliant news if you're in Mr Brunton's class: we've got a Baker Street Academy–themed writing project – but just to make things that little bit more interesting, I thought we could turn it into a short-story writing competition too?!

We could have a prize for the best ones! (Hopefully.) You'll even get to have it posted here on the Baker Street Blog.

So, what's it going to be? History? Action? Adventure? Thriller or Mystery? You decide!

 8 Comments

 Comments:
Mr Brunton: Marvellous stuff, John. A bit of enthusiasm; now that's what I like to see! I think this is a great idea! We might even be able to display your work in the new BSA Arts Wing once it's opened later this term! I hope everybody is excited about doing this creative work and I want you all to have some fun with it.

 Comments:
Anon: Oh man. Writing is hard! What are we supposed to write about anyway?

Comments:
Anon1: Yeah, do we have to write something about ourselves?

Comments:
NinjaKatz1: Does it have to be about Baker Street Academy? Can't it be about ninjas? Ninjas are awesome!

Comments:
NinjaKatz1: What about guinea pigs? My guinea pig is really funny.

Comments:
Mr Brunton: Baker Street Academy is just a starting point. I suppose it can be about anybody or anything you like! It would be wonderful to see some of you get stuck in and write a piece about Baker Street Academy itself though. I've been doing some research and I know the school has quite a fascinating history!

Failing that, I'm sure some of you might even like to think of something ghostly! Woooo! It is spooky season, after all...

Comments:
Anon1: John's good at stories. He can write about the Baker Street Ghost!

Comments:
Anon: Yeah or the Baker Street Curse. Ha ha ha! You're all doomed!

The next few days went by without any incidents. Probably a good job... Any more spookiness round here and I think some heads would pop!

We did get another bonus Mr Brunton lesson though; he was covering a Maths class for Mr Rishi so we all ended up outside again! This time he was getting us to think about trigonometry and how it can be used to work out the height of the buildings and trees around Baker Street Academy.

And Daz and Martin said they saw him outside another afternoon with a long stick of poles taped together, wobbling about all over the place and trying to chase the shadows! He really is funny!

Sherlock kept himself suspiciously quiet. He said he was doing some research for our Baker Street Academy project. Knowing him, he was busy working up some sort of deductive master plan for all the strangeness going on at school...

After-school clubs:

Monday:

Drama Club with Mrs Parker:

Learn the secrets of the stage! Theatrical make-up and effects.

Tuesday:

Spooky Science! with Mr Spice:

Create your own cobwebs, see the spooky smoke and make some ghostly slime!

4
BAKER STREET GHOSTS

DING DING

TING TING TING

BZZZZT!

SWOOOOSH!

BSA Social
online

Henry
OMG! We saw the Baker Street Academy
Ghost!
12:10

Emily
Yeah It was so scary!
12:10

Martha
No way! What happened?
12:10

Bart
It was at after school club! In the halls near
the Old Wing 😨
12:11

Martha
Mr Musgrave saw it in the Old Wing!
12:11

Daz
What did it look like!? I'd have run away like
sooooo quick.
12:12

Henry
It was, like, glowing in the dark…
12:12

Seb
Ahh, diddums! Scared of the dark, are we?
12:13

Charlie M
Boo hoo!
12:13

Martha
Ignore them, guys! Tell me more. Sherlock, are you seeing this?
12:13

Sherlock
Oh yes! Ghastly!
12:14

Martin
We could hear it moaning, like "Woooooooo!!" And footsteps and everything…
12:14

Sherlock
Oh yes, well, it must have been a ghost then!
12:14

Martin
It definitely was the ghost!

12:14

Seb
It's the curse!

12:15

Daz
He's joking… I think.

12:15

Seb
It's no joke. If you see the Baker Street Ghost, then you're cursed too!

12:15

Charlie M
Yeah, you'll disappear, ha ha! No one will know what happened to you!

12:16

Bart
Shut up!

12:16

Send

43

MR MUSGRAVE

THE BAKER STREET ACADEMY CARETAKER

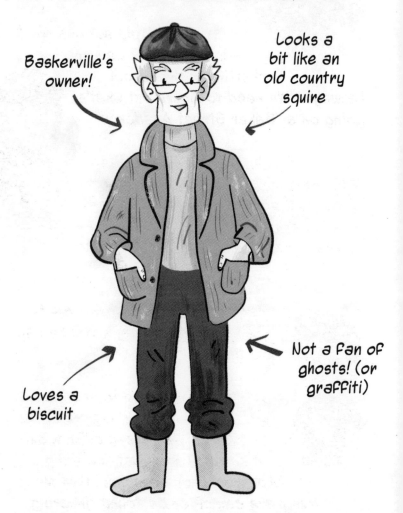

Baskerville's owner!

Looks a bit like an old country squire

Loves a biscuit

Not a fan of ghosts! (or graffiti)

What's going on? I'll tell you what's going on. Everything's gone crazy overnight again. That's what!

"This is getting serious now," said Martha as we were chatting in the school hallways. "We need to figure out what's going on at Baker Street Academy!"

"Funnily enough, I was just thinking the very same thing," agreed Sherlock. "I think we might just pay Mr Musgrave a visit. I think its time to have a look at what's been going on around the Old Wing."

"Yes!" said Martha. "Ooh - maybe he'll show us exactly where he saw the ghost?"

So we went off to see if we could find Mr Musgrave in his office. Well, I say office, but it's pretty much just like a big storeroom for the school that Mr Musgrave can often be found tinkering around in.

45

KNOCK
KNOCK

"Yes, yes, just a moment!" called Mr Musgrave. "Oh, it's you! Hello, Martha, Sherlock - ooh, and John too. Come in, come in. What can I do for you three then?"

"We wanna know more about the ghost!" Martha blurted out excitedly. "Sherlock doesn't believe it!"

"Martha! That's not quite right," said Sherlock. He was smiling though. He clearly had some idea of what he thought had been going on recently...

"Can you show us around the Old Wing, Mr Musgrave?" I asked, trying to help. "We thought you could help us find out about what's been going on."

"Yeah!" said Martha. "We definitely wanna see where you saw the ghost!"

Oh, not you lot as well! Ghost this! Curse that! That's all any of the kids have been talking about round here. And Mr Brunton has been in here quizzing me about it too! I'm getting a bit tired of it, to be honest with you: graffiti everywhere and all this silliness about the curse!

"So you're saying there is a 'curse' then, are you, Mr M?" said Martha hopefully.

"Of course not," said Mr Musgrave, more to himself than in reply to Martha. "It's nonsense! Well I always thought it was nonsense, but I suppose after the last few days, I'm not so sure..."

ADVENTURE
WITH THE
CARETAKER'S GHOST

After some mild grumbling, and a bit of
persuasion (a handy spare packet of my
bourbon biscuits!) Mr Musgrave said he'd show us
around the Old Wing of Baker Street Academy.
He was apprehensive, but I think secretly he
wanted to get to the bottom of it as much as we
did!

"Cor! It's really cool in here," said Martha, as we followed Mr Musgrave around the Old Wing's hallways. It had a completely different feel to the parts of Baker Street Academy that we were used to. "It's a bit like an old house or museum or something." I said. "Why isn't it used any more as part of the school?"

"It was, until not so long ago," said Mr Musgrave. "When I was small, this wing used to be the primary school! More recently there were adult education classes in the evenings, and they still use the Old Library for special occasions."

"But until the money had been raised for the renovations, it was mainly used as the school storage - here and the basement area underneath Baker Street Academy, I mean - but technically, the cellars are part of the old *Musgrave House*. And there's nothing to see down there, apart from decades of discarded school furniture and a few old log piles!"

"Did you say ...

MUSGRAVE HOUSE?"

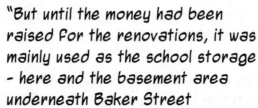

"That's right, Martha. Baker Street Academy wasn't always a school, you know. Before that, it used to be called Musgrave House! Well, this Old Wing part of it did, at least."

"Very interesting!" said Sherlock with a thoughtful look about him. I could tell his megabrain was clicking into gear.

"Wow!" said Martha. "Did you live here then, Mr Musgrave?"

"He he - not me, Martha! That was over a hundred and fifty years ago! The last Musgrave to live here was some sort of famous theatre actor, I think. I did go to school here though. The whole family did, in fact! And I remember my grandfather said there's been a Musgrave family around here for generations. Right the way back to King Charles the First!"

THE BAKER STREET/MUSGRAVE CURSE!

We followed Mr Musgrave round until we got to the Old Library. Wow, what an amazing room! It was lined with books in ancient wooden shelving and antique portrait paintings up around the walls. At one side was a great big fireplace and there were chairs, desks and tables dotted around for reading or studying.

Poor Mr Musgrave looked like he didn't really want to be in there.

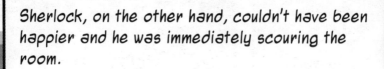

Sherlock, on the other hand, couldn't have been happier and he was immediately scouring the room.

"What exactly happened on the night you saw the 'ghost', Mr Musgrave?" asked Sherlock.

54

Yes, yes, and then what happened?

Well, I've never seen anything like it.

It was a ghost, I tell you – a man. He looked all old-fashioned too – sort of familiar.

Well, the light went out. And then he just – vanished, you know.

That's right! Well, I mean, I suppose I was a bit shocked, but he was there one minute. And he wasn't there the next. And I would've seen him leave otherwise; I know I would.

It was a strange light.

Amazing! But can you tell me what you observed?

Familiar, you say. Now, that is very important. Then what?

Vanished, you say?

Indeed!

55

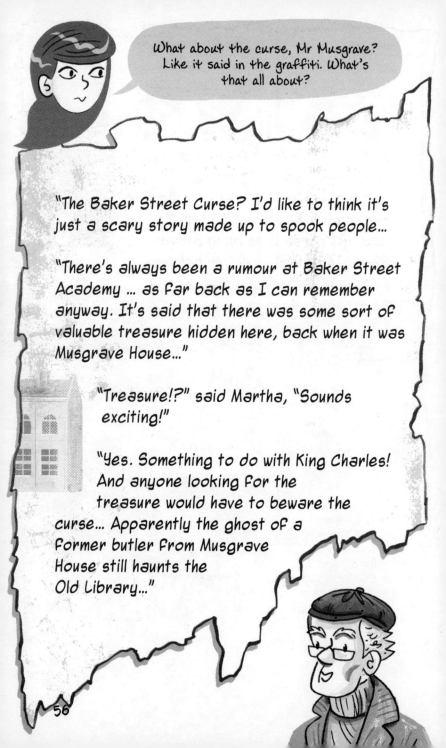

What about the curse, Mr Musgrave? Like it said in the graffiti. What's that all about?

"The Baker Street Curse? I'd like to think it's just a scary story made up to spook people...

"There's always been a rumour at Baker Street Academy ... as far back as I can remember anyway. It's said that there was some sort of valuable treasure hidden here, back when it was Musgrave House..."

"Treasure!?" said Martha, "Sounds exciting!"

"Yes. Something to do with King Charles! And anyone looking for the treasure would have to beware the curse... Apparently the ghost of a former butler from Musgrave House still haunts the Old Library..."

"That must be the Baker Street Ghost!?"

"Supposedly he went missing while looking for the treasure and was never seen again," continued Mr Musgrave. "To this very day, no one knows what happened to him. So now, the curse lives on in Baker Street Academy ... if you believe that sort of thing. I suppose it's become a bit like an old legend. Although not a very funny one recently..."

Just then a voice surprised us all:

Ooh! Missing treasures and a ghostly butler!

Now that really does sound like something we could work up for our Baker Street Academy stories this term, Mr Musgrave! Just the right kind of spooky, don't you think!?

"Mr Brunton! What are you doing in here!?" asked a very surprised Mr Musgrave. "You gave us quite a fright!"

"Oh ... I'm terribly sorry, Mr Musgrave. I didn't mean to... It's just that I've been so excited about the new Arts Wing, I wanted to have a nose around the building."

"Yes, well, you're not meant to be in here, Mr Brunton," said a cross-sounding Mr Musgrave. "If you really wanted to see how the Arts Wing is coming along, you only needed to ask me first and I'd've been glad to show you around. Right, I think that's enough for today! Come on, you lot. I've got work to be getting on with!"

...221B

"Hey, that was a bit weird, wasn't it!" said Martha when we got back home to 221B that afternoon. "I got spooked when Mr Brunton popped up out of nowhere in the old library... I thought it was the ghost!"

"I think Mr Musgrave did too, for a moment," replied Sherlock seriously "I think he's more worried than he wants to let on."

"What do you think Mr Brunton was doing?" I asked. "Hey - did you notice he was holding a map or something when he found us?"

"Well observed, John!" Sherlock flashed me a little smile "We'll make a detective of you yet! But that's not all. He had something else too - look, he dropped this." Sherlock pulled a slightly crumpled and fragile-looking scrap of paper out of his coat pocket. It was yellowing and old-looking with some sort of strange writing on it.

"Ooh, what is it?" asked Martha, grabbing it excitedly.

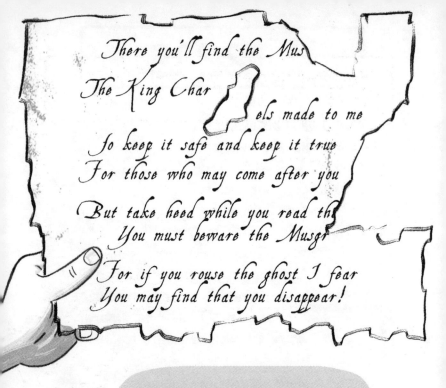

There you'll find the Mus
The King Char
els made to me
So keep it safe and keep it true
For those who may come after you

But take heed while you read th
You must beware the Musgr

For if you rouse the ghost I fear
You may find that you disappear!

It's a bit of weird poetry or something... I bet he just found it in the library?

Sherlock took the scrap of paper and started to examine it up close.

I don't think so, Martha. Look, there's some drawing on the back too... Very interesting.

"Hey, does that say Musgrave?" I said. "That's weird."

Musgrave Ha

It does indeed, John. It does indeed!

THE GAME'S AFOOT!

WOOF!

"Baskerville seems to like it, whatever it is!" laughed Martha.

"Baskerville has discerning taste! I think this calls for a little after-school adventure." Sherlock sprang up out of the chair and put the lead on a very waggy-tailed Baskerville. "Come on then, you two, get your coats! We're going back to school."

GOOD HEAVENS, SHERLOCK!

IT REALLY DOES SOUND LIKE THINGS ARE
GETTING A BIT MYSTERIOUS AT BAKER
STREET ACADEMY IN MY ABSENCE... EVEN
THE STUDENTS ARE SEEING GHOSTS!

I DO HOPE YOU AND YOUR CHUMS AREN'T
GETTING TOO SPOOKED. IT MUST BE THAT
TIME OF YEAR!

YOURS SHIVERINGLY,

M X

SHERLOCK HOLMES

221B BAKER STREET

LONDON

NW1 6XE

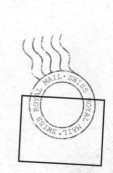

63

5

EXTRACURRICULAR

ACTIVITIES

64

It looked suspiciously like Sherlock had other plans as usual...

> After-school club sounds splendid, John. If you want to go to Spooky Science with Mr Spice, then be my guest! But I had another sort of 'after school' idea in mind for this evening. And besides, Baskerville needs his walkies, don't you, boy?

Sherlock took out the crumply bit of paper we'd found in the Old Wing and crouched down in front of Baskerville.

"Now what are you doing?" asked Martha.

"Just a moment!"

Sherlock shoved the paper under Baskerville's nose. He sniffed at it excitedly, then let out a little woof and suddenly we were off, being dragged this way and that
through the school corridors...

He definitely had the scent of something! I had a job to keep up with him as he led us all the way round the classrooms and halls ... straight to Mr Musgrave's storeroom office...

"Oh, Baskerville!" tutted Martha as we stopped outside. "He's probably just looking for Mr Musgrave!"

"Yeah, but the door's open," I pointed out. "That's a bit weird, right?"

Martha smiled. "Maybe we should have a look around?"

The room was a jumble of
all sorts of things as usual – shelves and
shelves of supplies, and whatever Mr Musgrave
was in the middle of putting away or needing to
fix. Baskerville pulled us straight over to a desk
absolutely covered in papers.

"He's found something in there he
likes!" said Martha.

Baskerville woofed
in agreement and started scratching at the
drawers on Mr Musgrave's desk.

"Quickly, open it up," whispered Sherlock.

"I think someone's coming..."

Martha opened the drawer and nearly burst out
laughing.

"Oh, Baskerville! Trust you to find something completely not useful! Hey look, everybody, we've stumbled across the world's biggest secret ... Mr Musgrave's biscuit drawer! I can't see how that's going to be much use!"

"Don't be so hasty, Martha," said Sherlock as he rummaged around on the desk and then in the drawer. "Hmm ... that's interesting. Ah! Now so is that! Oh, good boy, Baskerville. This will do nicely." Sherlock grabbed something, and we hurried out of the storeroom office just in time. It sounded like the after-school clubs had finished and it probably wasn't a good idea to be caught nosing around where we didn't belong.

"Hey, why don't we go and catch up with the guys after the clubs?"

"Not just yet, Martha," said Sherlock, waving his finger. "I don't think Baskerville's finished his walk for the evening!" Baskerville woofed in agreement and Sherlock dangled a set of keys up in front of us. "I thought we might have another look around the Old Wing."

Mr Musgrave's not going to be happy about that, I thought to myself. But the thought didn't last long, because just then...

JOHN WATSON **MARTHA HUDSON** **SHERLOCK HOLMES**

SHERLOCK HOLMES CHASES DEATH!

Aargh! I froze completely. Martha must've seen the look of terror on my face.

"What's the matter, John? Oh my g-"

Woof! Grrrr! Baskerville started pulling on the lead. In the gloom of the corridor ahead of us stood an eerily glowing figure...

69

"Wh-what should we do?"

"What should we do? Well, isn't it obvious? We catch it! Come on!"

Before Martha and I could even make a sound, let alone disagree, Sherlock was sprinting off after the ghostly figure that had appeared at the other end of the corridor. I was so stunned, I dropped Baskerville's lead and he shot off after Sherlock into the gloom...

In the time it took me and Martha to pull ourselves together and catch up with them, the strange apparition had gone... It had vanished! I mean, it just disappeared right before our eyes. It was unbelievable!

"OMG! That was definitely a ghost, Sherlock. You can't deny it now, can you?"

"Oh, I'm not denying it, Martha! In fact, I'd say it absolutely confirms what I've been thinking."

71

A GOOD DOG NOSE BEST

It was hard to know if we'd all been seeing things or if there really was something real and ghostly there in the school hallways... Whatever it was, it hadn't put Sherlock off in the slightest and we had to hurry to keep up with him. Sherlock used the keys we'd found in Mr Musgrave's office and we followed him back into the Old Wing of Baker Street Academy.

"What was that all about then, Sherlock?! You can't seriously tell me you don't believe in the ghost now, can you? And what do you mean, it confirms what you've been thinking?"

"No time for that right now, Martha. And I've told you already - there's no such thing as ghosts! Now shhh! We've got to be quiet; we definitely don't want to get caught in here."

"Especially not by whatever that was," I said. Or Mr Musgrave, for that matter, I thought.

Sherlock gave Baskerville another good iff of the piece of paper and he sniffed excitedly, pulling us this way and that through the gloomy dark corridors. It wasn't long before we ended up back in the Old Library.

"Back in here again!", said Martha, "where Mr Musgrave saw the ghost..."

Baskerville pulled us over to the grand fireplace on the far side of the room.

WOOF!

WOOF!

WOOF!

Shh, Baskerville. Good boy! I think he's found what he wants.

In the fireplace? How's that going to help?

"Let's take a look, shall we?" Sherlock stepped closer and stuck his head up into the fireplace. "I can't see much," he said. "Probably best not to use any lights." Then he reached in and scratched around up inside the chimney, until suddenly he let out a decisive "Ha!"

"What is it?" whispered Martha. "What have you found?"

Sherlock pulled out a smallish box, about the size of a shoebox. He blew the dust off the top and put it down on the nearest desk, carefully lifting the lid... "Good boy, Baskerville. I knew you had it in you. Never doubted you for a second!"

"Let me see! Let me see! Oh ... it's just a box full of paper!" Martha sounded a little disappointed.

"What were you expecting?" asked Sherlock.

"I don't know! Treasure?! Something exciting! What's on it?"

"Watson it what?" I said.

"Tut. Not Watson, *John!* I can't see what's on it."

Without any light, it was hard to make out exactly what was in the box, but it looked like it might be more of the same strange poem Sherlock had found earlier...

BASKERVILLE
IN... GHOST WATCH!

OK, readers, we're on the lookout here in the darkness at Baker Street Academy, ready for anything that might just try and go bump in the night! We've got a packed lunch, our spooky water and our cameras ready. Everybody set? Recording ... now!

WOOOOO!

There! Oh my goodness! What was that?

AWOOOOO! AWOOOOO!

Oh, there it is again! Aargh! Something just brushed my leg!

WOOOOOOOO! WOOOOOOOF!

Wait a minute... Ghosts don't woof! Quick, turn on the lights!

AWOOO - WOOF!

Oh, Baskerville!

6
The Musgrave Riddle

Once a great prize did belong
To one who has now long been gone

And now there must be someone new
To find the prize and keep it true

First one must observe the sun
Above the Old Oak in time for one

Follow the shadow where it falls
Under the Elm into the halls

Go on past birch and chestnut tree
Then look west to discover thee

Find the ancestral Musgrave town
Then look behind and follow down

There you'll find the Musgrave Treasure
The King Charles Crown Jewels made to measure

So keep it safe and keep it true
For those who may come after you

But take heed whilst you read this verse
You must beware the Musgrave Curse

For if you rouse the ghost I fear
You may find that you disappear!

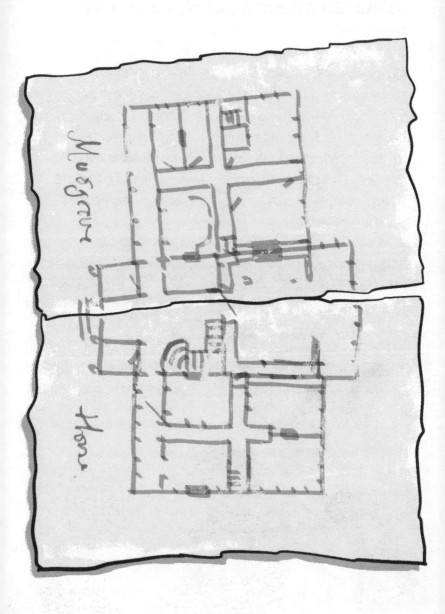

"Blimey, that is one weird poem!" said Martha. "But I like it! Especially the bit about treasure!"

My guess was right. Once we had a chance to properly examine the contents of the box Sherlock found in the fireplace, it did seem to be more of the same strange writing that was on the scrap that we found in the Old Library earlier. Only now, it looked like we had the whole thing, complete with a plan or map of some kind on the reverse.

"King Charles' crown jewels... Didn't Mr Musgrave mention something about a king? I wonder what it's all about?"

"It's like a puzzle, or a riddle, isn't it?" I said. "And that definitely says Musgrave. No two ways about it this time! What do you think, Sherlock?"

"Well, you're right about it being a riddle, John." Sherlock waggled his finger at me. "And it is actually a puzzle by the looks of it. It's old too - but there's no date. What do you think?"

"I don't know," I said, trying hard to think like Sherlock would, as I examined the paper. "It looks like it could be from sometime around the 17th century?"

"How would you know?" said Martha cheekily.

"The spelling," I pointed out. "If you look here - these big Fs are actually S. It's how they used to write back then! I remember seeing some stuff like this at the B&A museum."

"Haha! Fuper!" giggled Martha. "What fplendid deductions, John!"

"Oh, ftop it!" said Sherlock, laughing too. "This is ferious ftuff you know!

"Ha ha! And that's not a bad try, actually, John - but in this case you're out by a couple of centuries. The writing is definitely meant to look old, but the paper is clearly from the late 19th century. You can see here from the watermark."

"Yeah, but what does it mean?" I asked. "Why would someone do that? What's the Musgrave treasure? And what's it got to do with the stuff that's been going on at Baker Street Academy? And how does Mr Musgrave fit into all this?"

Well it should be simple enough, John. There's nothing better than a good puzzle! All we need to do is work out how to solve it! And I think I have a good idea of how to start...

Tut! Typical Sherlock. Simple plus puzzle usually added up to brain boggling for the rest of us!

SHERLOCK **HOLMES** & JOHN **WATSON**

THE

CLASSROOM OF

FEAR

"WHAT TERRORS AWAIT INSIDE?"

Tremble in fear, dear readers! Where once you were on the enlightened path of mystery, now you must tread the creaky boards of terror! Watch helplessly as the treacly fingers of doom close in! Feel the hairs stand on the back of your neck! Shiver with fright as the tingle climbs up your spine...

And now imagine, dear reader. Imagine yourself in the infinite darkness. Alone with only your innermost thoughts as company. Pray they don't betray you!

Who's that breathing down the back of your neck? Dare you turn and face the horror? How long have you been down in the blackness? Something's coming, ever closer as the light slowly fades. You can hear its breath. Jaws salivating, teeth dripping...

> Bravo, John! An excellent reading! Well done. You really had everybody on the edge of their seats. I think that one's going to be hard to top. OK, who's up next?

Mr Brunton had let us run with the idea of coming up with some short stories. And after the strange events around here recently, I couldn't help but almost scare myself with thoughts of something spooky! Not everybody seemed to be feeling the same way though...

Em and Nisha both wrote about their favourite place to go on holiday: New York, because it was like a movie set! And Martin actually did write about ninjas. Cat ninjas! It was pretty funny!

Daz lost his story (who would've guessed!?).

> My mum washed it!

But I think Sherlock surprised everybody the most when he decided to stand up in class and dramatically read out the strange "Musgrave Riddle" we'd found during our after-school investigations. I certainly wasn't expecting it - and I don't think anybody else knew what to make of it, judging by their expressions. Mr Brunton however, was absolutely thrilled. I don't think I'd seen him quite as excited as that - and that's saying something!

Excellent work, Sherlock, that really is some fascinating stuff! Where did you find that, I wonder?! I can't wait to take a good look at it later.

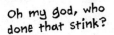

Bart was up next, not that anybody was paying attention by that point as a particularly nasty smell had started wafting around the room...

PHWOAR!!

Oh my god, who done that stink?

Darren. Ha ha!

Ha ha! John's story wasn't that scary!

Koff!

Koff!

Kaff!

Splatter!

Within seconds the classroom was filling with acrid green smoke. People were laughing at first – I mean, it did seem kind of funny, especially as some of us were trying to creep each other out.

Oh my god! This is pretty spooky!

It's like a ghost movie!

Koff! It stinks!

I can't breathe!
Someone open a
window.

But the laughter turned to fright almost as quickly
when an eerie voice started to speak over the
school tannoy...

YOU HAVE
BEEN WARNED!

BEWARE
THE BAKER STREET
GHOST!

BEWARE
THE BAKER STREET
CURSE!

89

petition too?!

We could have a prize for the best ones! (Hopefully) You'll even get to have it posted here on the Baker Street Blog.

So, what's it going to be? History? Action? Adventure? Thriller or Mystery? You decide!

School Closing Temporarily
Today 15:34

Dear BSA students,

Due to the events of yesterday afternoon and the rather unseemly nature of recent incidents at Baker Street Academy, we are sorry to announce that the school will be closing early this week so that everything can be brought back to order. We hope to be open again as soon as possible. The safety of staff and pupils at the school must be of paramount importance.

Any remaining work in the Old Wing of the academy will also cease until the school has reopened and the administration is able to reorganize the contractors on site.

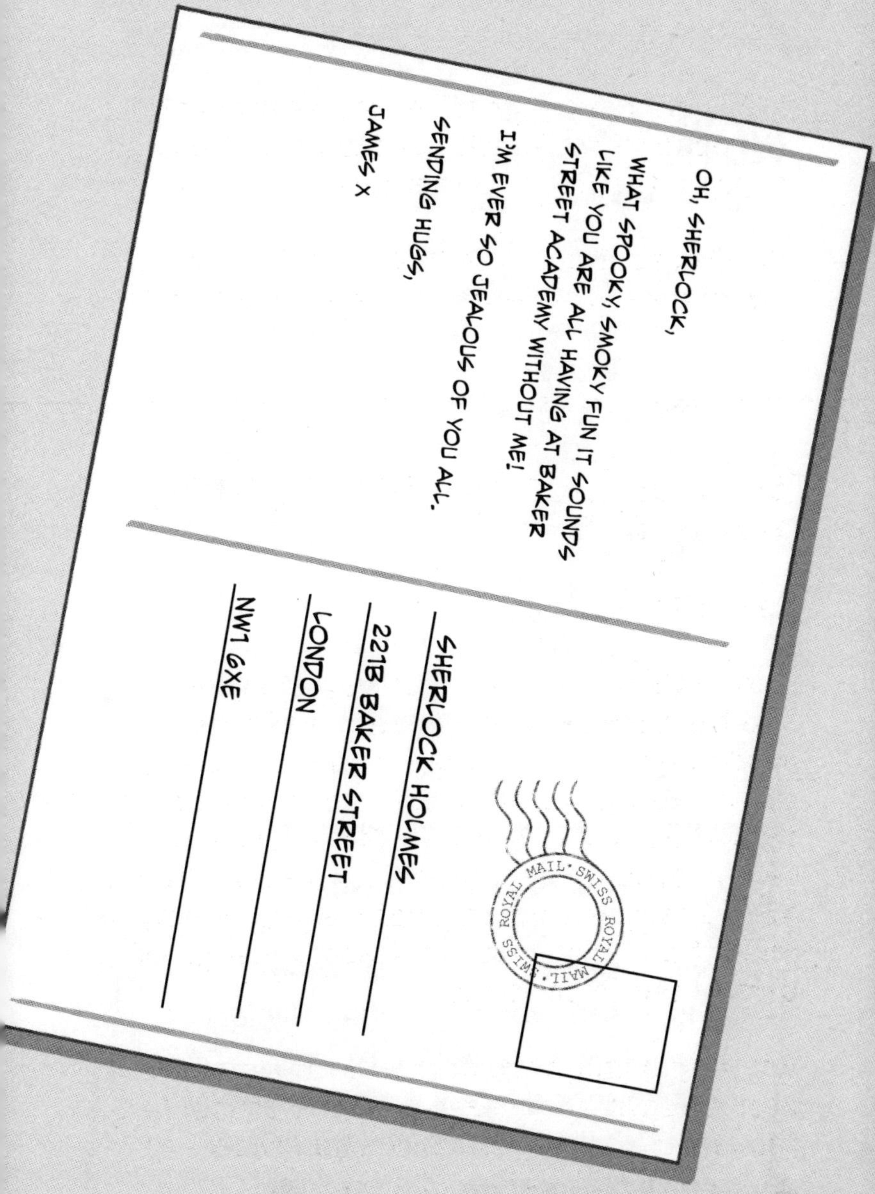

OH, SHERLOCK,

WHAT SPOOKY, SMOKY FUN IT SOUNDS
LIKE YOU ARE ALL HAVING AT BAKER
STREET ACADEMY WITHOUT ME!

I'M EVER SO JEALOUS OF YOU ALL.

SENDING HUGS,

JAMES X

SHERLOCK HOLMES

221B BAKER STREET

LONDON

NW1 6XE

ROYAL MAIL · SWISS ROYAL
MAIL · SWISS

91

7 GHOSTLY GOINGS ON

WOW... It didn't seem like that particular kind of weirdness was brewing at school, but I guess you never can tell these days at Baker Street Academy! For Martha, it was just the confirmation she needed and she was determinedly buzzing around our 221B living room saying things like:

You see, John? Sherlock's crazy for not believing in ghosts!

and

I knew Mr Musgrave really did see something spooky!

I wasn't sure what to make of it all, but if school was shut, it must've been serious... I suppose it's an understatement to say that the last few weeks have been a bit crazy. I know Sherlock loves a riddle, but why can't school be normal like it is for everyone else?

Not that we saw much of Sherlock! He wasted no time in saying he had other things he wanted to look into. Maybe he was getting help from his super-intelligent brother, Mycroft? (Yep, I know, it's a weird name! But then, so is Sherlock, right?!) Whatever he was up to, Martha and I tried to make the most of the extra free time and we went for a look around the B&A museum.

MYCROFT?

When we got back to 221B something very strange was going on... The front room was a mess. And it smelled decidedly eggy.

"Sherlock! What are you doing?" The dining table had been commandeered by Sherlock and looked like it was covered in kitchen utensils from Mrs Hudson's cupboards. And half of the science stock cupboards from school...

Just a little experiment, John. In this case, some cabbagey water, a helping of dry ice, a drop of ammonia, some green food colouring, a few jars and our science textbook. You'd be surprised at what you can come up with using a few easily available implements. Well, at least I think I can come up with it...

When did you get all this stuff?

Yeah, won't Mr Spice be missing a few things?

I'm certain he won't mind. Especially if I get this... Yes... That should do it!

Sherlock poured a beaker of green stuff into a bubbling jar of something stinky. The mixture made a flumping noise and, in an instant, the room was filled with smelly green smoke - just like in the classroom at school!

"Very interesting," said Sherlock, as he waved his arms around to clear some of the stinky smoke. "Very spooky!"

Yep, you guessed it. Before Martha and I were enlightened as to what was so very interesting, or very spooky, Sherlock's pocket pinged, and a few moments later he was striding towards the door.

"There's something I need to look into!"

THE SILVERY BLAZER

Q: Who knows what goes on in Sherlock's head when he's having one of his brainwaves?

A: Not me!

Martha and I tried our best to clean the living room, and by the time Sherlock reappeared back at Mrs Hudson's house, he had a very satisfied look about him, and an interesting addition to his wardrobe... Sherlock was wearing what appeared to be a sparkly silver blazer.

"Wow, that's a jazzy number, Sherlock." Martha was being cheeky.

Quite, Martha! Fortunately, this is not my new styling choice for the season.

I hadn't noticed that Sherlock was shining his phone light on to the jacket; as he turned it off, the shimmer faded and it looked like any ordinary dark blazer. If a bit too big.

"Aw, that's a shame," said Martha, "I needed a good laugh! What're you wearing it for anyway?"

"Well, that is the interesting thing!" To demonstrate, Sherlock turned out the lights and disappeared into his bedroom. After a few

CLUNKS and CLANKS,

he must've found what he was looking for, because there was a triumphant "Ha!" and, moments later...

An eerily glowing presence emerged from his room...

OMG,
what is going on?

Martha nearly jumped out of her skin. In the darkness, it looked almost like the Baker Street Ghost was there, in the living room!

I switched the lights back on and there was Sherlock, standing with a big grin on his face, swinging an old-fashioned lantern.

"I did say it was interesting!" he said, blowing out the light. Once again, the jacket lost its shimmer and looked very ordinary.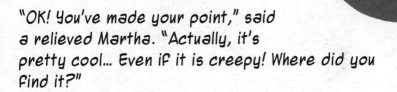

"OK! You've made your point," said a relieved Martha. "Actually, it's pretty cool... Even if it is creepy! Where did you find it?"

"Well, that's interesting too - I picked it up at school this afternoon. I've been taking advantage of a closed Baker Street Academy to make further investigations into Mr Musgrave and our new teacher, Mr Brunton. I think you could say I've made some interesting developments!"

Sherlock said he'd found the jacket, along with a smoke machine and make-up props, in Mr Musgrave's office - and that they hadn't been there when we were searching the other night. He went on to explain how the spooky experiment he'd set up in the living room earlier could be enhanced with the smoke machine, and that the jacket's reflective material would give off a ghostly glow if lit with the right sort of light in the correct circumstances. I think what he was saying is that he believed he'd found some answers to whoever or whatever was behind the recent events and appearance of the

BAKER STREET GHOST.

It definitely sounded suspicious, even if Martha was convinced there was still something otherworldly going on at school.

> Jeez. What is it with Baker Street Academy and all the weirdness? Do you think Mr Musgrave is hiding something? Do you think he could be behind some of the strange goings-on at Baker Street Academy?! Don't tell me Mr Brunton's not all he's cracked up to be as well, is he?

"I think the answers will come soon enough," said Sherlock. "It's a singular problem!"

incidents at Baker Street Academy, we are sorry to announce that the school will be closing early this week so that everything can be brought back to order. We hope to be open again as soon as possible. The safety of staff and pupils at the school must be of paramount importance.

Work in the Old Wing of the academy will also cease until the school has reopened and the administration is able to reorganize the contractors on site.

Baker Street Announcement
Today 09:20

Dear BSA students,

We are happy to announce that school will be open again as normal from tomorrow morning. We look forward to seeing you all bright and early!

Once again, we would like to apologize for the enforced closure over the last few days and hope that it has not caused too much inconvenience.

Mrs Cavendish, BSA Headteacher.

MISSING

Good morning, everybody! It's been quite a strange few days, but I'm sure none of you will be complaining about some extra time off! I'm afraid Mr Brunton hasn't made it in today - so I'll be covering in his absence.

Nobody minded having Mr Gapp instead of Mr Brunton at school that morning. Sherlock thought it was a bit odd though - apparently all Mr Brunton's things were there in the classroom when we'd arrived, like his bag, coat and computer and stuff - all laid out on the desk like he'd had to go out suddenly.

Where's Mr Brunton then, sir?

Yeah. Isn't that his bag and coat? I thought you said he wasn't coming in?

It's the curse! I told you it was true. He's disappeared!

Woooo!

Oh stop it, you two!

Hey, Darren's not in either - didn't he see the ghost the other day?

No. Darren's at the dentist. He lost his tooth! Ha ha!

Wow... Charlie and Seb decided to go all out on being extra, super annoying. They really turned it up a notch.

OH DEAR! POOR, POOR MR BRUNTON.

HE MUST'VE HAD A TERRIBLE FRIGHT.

WOOO! THE GHOST OF BAKER STREET ACADEMY HAS STRUCK AGAIN!

I WONDER WHERE HE COULD BE?

SEARCH ME! HA HA!

YEAH, I'M IN THE DARK ABOUT IT TOO, CHARLIE. HA HA! I THINK HE MUST'VE COME DOWN WITH SOMETHING!

MAYBE SUPERSTAR SCHOOLBOY DETECTIVE, SHERLOCK, CAN GET TO THE BOTTOM OF IT?

3 PART PROBLEM

I thought that things might have calmed down a bit at Baker Street Academy after a couple of days off, but no such luck! No one seemed to know what was going on and things were just as confusing as ever - even more so, now that Mr Brunton had gone **AWOL**. I had a feeling that Sherlock was the only one around here who might have the answers...

"What's going on?" I asked, when Sherlock, Martha and I could find a minute to ourselves. "We've got **GHOSTS** at Baker Street Academy, we've found an old nonsense riddle - and now it looks like our new teacher has gone **MISSING!** It's just too crazy!

"Well, that's just the thing, John; what looks like three different sets of problems are really just parts of one bigger puzzle - and I think that

The Musgrave Riddle

is the key to unlocking the mystery!"

"The Musgrave Riddle?"

Martha looked at Sherlock quizzically. "You think that's going to tell us why Baker Street Academy has become **SPOOK CENTRAL** and why Mr Brunton hasn't come back to school?"

"But how do we make sense of it? And where do we start?" I asked. "It's all so confusing!"

"Yeah," agreed Martha. "It doesn't matter how many times we read through it, we still can't work out what it means! "

"We start at the beginning, of course," said Sherlock. "Find the data! Follow the clues!"

"But *how?*"

"We need to go and see Mr Musgrave again," said Sherlock. "I think it's about time we had a historical discussion! I've an idea as to what's been going on here, and a feeling that time is most definitely of the essence!"

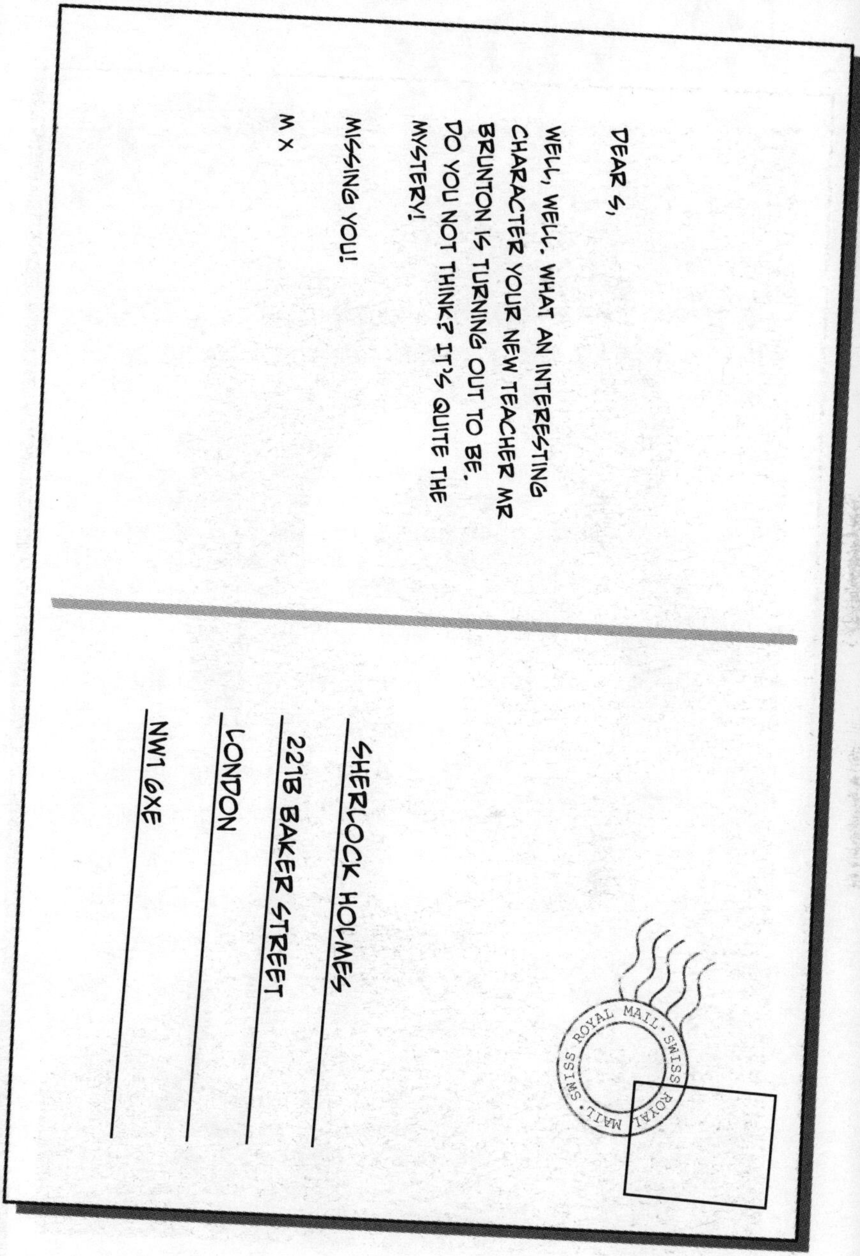

DEAR S,

WELL, WELL. WHAT AN INTERESTING
CHARACTER YOUR NEW TEACHER MR
BRUNTON IS TURNING OUT TO BE.
DO YOU NOT THINK? IT'S QUITE THE
MYSTERY!

MISSING YOU!

M X

SHERLOCK HOLMES

221B BAKER STREET

LONDON

NW1 6XE

SWISS ROYAL MAIL · SWISS ROYAL MAIL

8 RIDDLE ME THIS

The Musgrave Riddle?
Well I never!

Sherlock had shown Mr Musgrave a copy of the riddle and he had a serious face on as he read it over.

So this is what all the fuss has been about, eh? And you think that this is connected with the Baker Street Curse and what's been happening at Baker Street Academy?

"I'm certain of it, Mr Musgrave!" Sherlock had that excited twinkle in his eyes, the kind he gets when a problem is really buzzing round in his brain. "Ghosts, spookiness and a missing Mr Brunton. The riddle is the key!"

Hmmn. There are still some odd goings-on at school, you know, Sherlock. Last night, Mrs Musgrave heard howls coming from the school grounds! Howls! It was most disturbing...

What do you make of the riddle, Mr Musgrave? Does it mean anything to you?

Oh yes! I don't think I've seen it written down before, Sherlock, but it's very familiar. And you're not the first people to ask me about something like this, you know. Mr Brunton asked me about the very same thing!

"As I suspected!" said Sherlock.

It sounds just like a rhyme that my grandfather used to tell us when we were children... I remember, he used to say that his grandfather had told him and that it was a Musgrave family tradition. Yes! D'you know, I'd almost forgotten! He used to say it was all about Baker Street Academy – a bit like the old stories I told you about. My brothers and I would play along with it at school, but it was just a game. It never seemed to mean anything or lead anywhere, I'm sure of it!

If you don't mind, Mr Musgrave, I have to say that Mr Brunton has been a lot cleverer than any of us has realized!

"What do you mean, Sherlock?" I asked.

"Listen to the riddle, John:"

> *Once a great prize did belong*
> *To one who has now long been gone*
>
> *And now there must be someone new*
> *To find the prize and keep it true.*

It's clear that it's trying to tell us something important has been hidden safely whilst it waits for a new Musgrave to claim ownership.

"But why on earth would Mr Brunton be interested in it?" asked Mr Musgrave.

Yeah - are you saying he's worked out the riddle?

"Exactly that, Martha! And if we want some answers as to what's been going on around here, we must do the same! Look here..." Sherlock jabbed his finger at the lines on the page:

> *First one must observe the sun*
> *Above the Old Oak in time for one*

"I don't think it should be too difficult to get started!"

ADVENTURE
WITH THE
MUSGRAVE
?? RIDDLE ??

"I'm still of the opinion that it doesn't mean anything!" said Mr Musgrave as we got outside into the school grounds. "There's the Baker Street Academy oak tree over there - you can't miss it! But I'm telling you, we used to play along when we were children and it just doesn't lead anywhere!

"We shall see!" Sherlock positioned himself under the giant oak and scrutinized the Musgrave Riddle. "Now then, where were we?"

Follow the shadow where it falls
Under the elm into the halls

"What about an elm tree, Mr Musgrave? Was there ever one of those close by?"

"Hmm... I think there's a big stump from one on the other side of the grounds. There must have been a few more around, but they would have all perished from Dutch Elm disease."

"Hey, this is just like when we had lessons outside with Mr Brunton!" said Martha.

"That's crazy!" I agreed. "Do you think he was doing the same thing?"

Unfortunately, it looked like Mr Musgrave was right. Even though we found the remains of an elm tree, it didn't seem to be any help. We tried as best as we could to make some sense of the riddle and follow the steps around the school grounds, but it was useless. We just ended up somewhere in the middle of the playground every time!

"What about underneath the school?!" I suggested. "It says something about going down. We could try the basement?"

"An excellent idea, John!"

But again, it was a dead end. When Mr Musgrave had said it was all just full of old school junk and log piles, he wasn't joking. The rooms weren't even very big! And Mr Musgrave said there was no use worrying about what was under the playground, as it had all been dug up a few years back for resurfacing.

"There has to be something we're missing!" said Sherlock. He had his deep-thinking face on and he was pacing around the playground counting out measurements. "There must be a different oak and elm."

"What do you mean?" I said. "We've tried to follow the riddle..."

"There are lots of different trees in the grounds," Sherlock pointed out, "and the riddle mentions them too - ash, birch, chestnut."

"Sounds a bit like my old classrooms, now you mention it," said Mr Musgrave. "All the rooms in the Old Wing had different names; ever since it was Musgrave House, I think? I was in Acorn myself, but I remember Elm and Chestnut for sure!"

"Splendid!" said Sherlock rubbing his hands together. "Now we're getting somewhere! What of the 'old oak', I wonder? Think, Mr Musgrave, think!"

115

"There wasn't another old oak, Sherlock... Not as far as I can remember. But it's funny you should ask..."

"Yes? What is it? Remember!"

"Mr Brunton asked the same thing just the other week... The only thing I can think of which fits, is the building that used to be a pub across the road; that was called the Old Oak Inn."

"The Old Oak Inn!" said Sherlock! "Ha! Everything fits perfectly! That only leaves us a little while to get ready!"

"Get ready for what, Sherlock?"

"The sun. At one, of course!" And with that, Sherlock strode off back towards the school with a satisfied look.

SHERLOCK, SHERLOCK!

IT REALLY IS QUITE THE RIDDLE
YOU'VE GOT YOURSELF MIXED UP IN,
ISN'T IT?
DO YOU NEED SOME HELP, OR DO YOU
THINK YOU CAN MANAGE ALL ON YOUR
OWN? HEHE!

WISHING I COULD BE THERE,

JAMES X

SHERLOCK HOLMES

221B BAKER STREET

LONDON

NW1 6XE

ROYAL MAIL · SWISS ROYAL MAIL · SWISS

117

String Theory

Ten minutes later, Sherlock came back outside with a bunch of sports field flagpoles, some heavy-duty tape and a big ball of string. He immediately started fixing the poles together, until he had a long wobbly stick pointing upwards into the sky.

"Now what are you doing?" I asked

"'Follow the shadow where it falls
Under the elm into the halls'

"I'm making progress, John! The riddle clearly suggests to follow a shadow from the direction of the Old Oak Inn building, under an elm tree. As we've only got a stump left of the elm, I'll have to use this stick instead and take a height reference from the other trees, but it should help to get us where we need to be!"

"I can tell you the height of the elm!" said Mr Musgrave. "It was sixty-four feet; we had to work that out at school when I was here, you know! Trigonometry, I think it was."

"Trigonometry? Just like the other lesson with Mr Brunton! That's weird!"

"Yeah - and didn't Daz and Martin say they saw him out here chasing shadows around one day too?!"

"Excellent news!" said Sherlock. "That should only leave a simple calculation to get the desired effect."

After making a note of the length of shadow from the poles, Sherlock stretched a long piece of string across the playground. As we got to the end of the measurement, it had taken us over to the Old Wing of Baker Street Academy.

"Ha! Look here," said Sherlock, pointing at a chalk mark on the ground just inches from us. "We are definitely on the right trail! Looks like we need to go into the building. If you don't mind, Mr Musgrave, I'd like you to tell me which classroom was which!"

A VISIT TO

THE LIBRARY

Once Sherlock had an idea of where he needed to go, Mr Musgrave left us to make sense of the rest of the riddle back in the Old Wing of Baker Street Academy.

"OK. What next?" I asked.

"Go on past Birch and Chestnut tree, John! That's what's next!" said Sherlock, waving the riddle at me.

Then 'look west to discover thee'?

Precisely, Martha! You're getting the picture!

Sherlock set off again at a pace; he was in his bloodhound mode, hot on the trail of the problem wrapped up in this mysterious Musgrave Riddle. We followed him through the corridors, past the former classrooms, and it led us straight back to...

The Old Library!

120

Again!? This place is Spook Central!

What are we looking for in here?

We're still following the riddle. 'Find the ancestral Musgrave town'...

But what does that even mean?

It means the Musgraves are one of the oldest families in Britain.

Sherlock was eagerly scouring the bookshelves.

Mostly they were in the north of England, but there was a branch of the family that made its way down to this part of the country some time in the late 17th century. It would seem Musgrave House was established in the 19th century though...

121

"Tut! Sherlock, you're doing that thing again," said Martha.

"What thing?"
"You know - that thing where we have no idea what you're on about, or how you know all this stuff!"

"Well, that's easy!" he said, still busily scanning the bookshelves. "While you and John have been worrying about ghosts, I've been doing my research."

"Sherlock! You're such a big head!"

"Nothing wrong with being a big head, Martha. And nothing wrong with a bit of history either. The Musgraves really are quite an interesting family. Besides,

123

there's a date etched into the fireplace mantle. It says: 1879."

"Still a big head!" grinned Martha.

"Aha! Now that's interesting," said Sherlock. "You see?"

"See what?" I asked. Sherlock had stopped suddenly in front of a shelf of books that looked pretty much like every other example in the room.

"That desk!"

"What about it?" asked Martha. "Not the actual desk, Martha. It wasn't here like this before, wedged up against the bookshelves.

Someone has moved it there on purpose!" Sherlock heaved the desk away from the shelf and flung himself down on to the floor, his nose almost touching the boards as he ran his hands along them. Underneath the shelves there was a large curving mark scratched across the floorboards. "Ha! Just as I hoped."

In one smooth motion, Sherlock sprang back to his feet and theatrically started examining the wall of books. He picked and pulled and hmmmed his way along them until he let out a satisfied, "Yes! This is exactly what I was looking for." He tugged on a large leather-bound volume and with a soft click, a section of the bookcase started to come away from the wall and swung out into the room...

"NO WAY!"

said Martha,

"I can't believe you've found a door in a bookcase!"

"Way!" said Sherlock, grinning happily.

"And it's a way in, actually," he added matter-of-factly. "It's a doorway down to the cellars underneath the very oldest part of Baker Street Academy, or, as we know now, Musgrave House!"

"How did you know that was there?!" I asked, astonished.

It was a calculation, John. I knew there must be a space that was hidden somehow; I'd measured the length of the rooms from outside and it didn't match the cellar we searched with Mr Musgrave. It's all in the riddle - 'Find the ancestral Musgrave town' - the small northern town where the original Musgrave family hail from, before their descendants came to London, is called Hurlstone. It was then I realized I'd seen a set of books on the Old Library shelves, linked to the Musgrave family. Sure enough, there was one titled The Musgraves of Hurlstone. And now here we are!

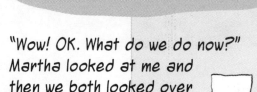

"Wow! OK. What do we do now?" Martha looked at me and then we both looked over at Sherlock.

"We do as we're told!" he said, and pointed at the riddle in his hand.

"We look behind and follow down, of course!"

Same old Sherlock.

He always sees the light,

while we scrabble around in
the darkness.

Always looking to take the
next step ...

... into adventure...

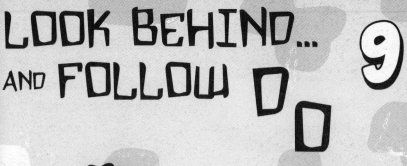

LOOK BEHIND... AND FOLLOW DOWN 9

And that bit about stepping into adventure... I just wish it wasn't mixed up with the inevitable trouble!

OOOOOOOH!

See what I mean?

131

We made our way down into the darkness and along a passage of some kind. I had a horrible feeling we weren't alone...

Ugh! Spiders! What exactly are we looking for?

Answers, Martha. Do keep up!

Someone's been here before us. Look.

Footprints?!

Indeed! This way.

133

The passageway finished, and the space opened out as we followed the light from the phone.

Whoa!

It's a secret room?!

This is amazing!

Elementary, John! It's exactly what I expected to find

through a secret door and down a secret passage!

It was hard to make out the details in the gloom, but it seemed like we were directly underneath the Old Library. As Sherlock swung the light around I could make out various bulky objects covered by dustsheets.

I wonder how many years it's been hidden away like this?

CRUNCH!

What was that?

Helloooo?

135

Glasses? And a broken phone... That's weird.

Someone's definitely been here.

I don't like it. Sort of feels a bit... I dunno... Ghoulish

Interesting choice of words, Martha, but there are no ghouls down here! Most houses definitely have their own personalities though. Much like the people that live in them... Like this! Ha!

Sherlock had pulled a dustsheet off what looked like an antique portrait painting. He shone the torch down at it.

137

"He looks like royalty," said Martha, excitedly. "Mr Musgrave will be amazed! He might be rich... Hey, wait! I've just remembered what it says in the riddle next; there you'll find..."

THE MUSGRAVE TREASURE!

THE KING CHARLES CROWN JEWELS!

IS THAT WHAT'S DOWN HERE!?

One step ahead of you, Martha.

Sherlock aimed the light over to where a cover had been pulled back, revealing an old wooden chest, with the lid opened.

"It looks like Mr Brunton did manage to unravel the Musgrave Riddle after all."
Wow!
Ooooohhh... Heeeelp!
Hang on, how do you know it was Mr Brunton?
OMG. It *IS* the ghost!
Sherlock?! Please tell me you can hear that?
Martha!
Somehow I don't think ghosts ask for help
What? You don't mean...

At the far end of the cellar, under a chink of light, sat a very distressed and dishevelled-looking Mr Brunton.

Out of The Cellar

With Mr Musgrave's help, we managed to pull Mr Brunton out from the secrets and gloom of the cellar. He looked decidedly the worse for wear.

Oh my goodness...

After all the searching... Finally found the Musgrave Treasure...

I just had to know...

The Musgrave Treasure?! What on earth is going on, Mr Brunton? What were you doing down there?

"If you don't mind," interrupted Sherlock eagerly, "I think I have the facts at hand to be able to fill in the details. It really is a most singular story!"

Mr Brunton here had a secret motive for taking a teaching position at Baker Street Academy. **A SECRET MOTIVE** that involved trying to unravel an **OLD FAMILY MYSTERY.** A mystery involving a **VICTORIAN RELATIVE,** who once worked as a *butler* at **MUSGRAVE HOUSE** and who was rumoured to have mysteriously *gone missing* whilst searching for a **HIDDEN TREASURE.** A hidden treasure of some significant importance, perhaps even of *royal* importance. Does any of that sound familiar?

"It sounds like the story Mr Musgrave told us about the Baker Street Curse," I said, "and the treasure seems the same as what's mentioned in the Musgrave Riddle!"

Exactly right, John! As I suspected, everything that has happened recently at Baker Street Academy has been wrapped up in the Musgrave Riddle. And Mr Brunton has been involved all along."

"But why?" asked Mr Musgrave. "This does all sound very much like the things my grandfather told me about Baker Street Academy. Isn't that strange?"

Not strange at all, Mr Musgrave! It appears you and Mr Brunton share much of the same history, although from different sides! We know that Mr Brunton has been trying to solve the Musgrave Riddle; indeed, he has solved the Musgrave Riddle, for the most part. But what's more interesting is the connection here... The infamous missing butler of **Musgrave House**, and as legend has it, the **Ghost of Baker Street Academy**, was none other our Mr Brunton's distant relative... **Mr Richard Brunton**. Is that not right, sir?

"The Musgrave House missing butler!? A Brunton? Well, I never!"

"OMG. Was that the skeleton? That's so creepy!"

"Whoa!"

144

WHAT THE BUTLER SAW

As we listened to Sherlock's excited explanation of the circumstances, Mr Brunton had started to come to his senses.

> Yes... Very good, Sherlock. And right, for the most part, although why it's anybody else's business is another thing. There was a story about one of my distant relatives and a treasure at Musgrave House... I assumed it was just a ghost story, but that changed when I discovered a copy of the Musgrave Riddle in some family possessions... When I started to research the Musgrave family history, I realized I may have stumbled upon something of true historical value. It completely changed everything! And now I'm the one who's found the Musgrave Treasure – the King Charles Crown Jewels!

> King Charles Crown Jewels?! I said that painting we found looked like royalty! That's amazing!

Not exactly, Martha.

"This is incredible, Sherlock!" Mr Musgrave looked dumbfounded. "But why go to such secretive lengths to get to the bottom of it all, Mr Brunton? What did you expect to achieve?"

Achieve? Ha! I just had to find out if the story was true! I just couldn't let it get the better of me... Had I not ended up trapped down in that HORRIBLE cellar, it would be a DIFFERENT story now, but I couldn't get out. The door was blocked... Those silly boys!

Silly boys?

I think he means Charlie and Seb.

Oh no - that's why the desk was wedged up against the bookcase in the library!

Then I fell and broke my glasses... I thought I was done for...

Pah! I'd have been gone and away with the Musgrave Treasure and none of you would have been the wiser!

I wouldn't be so sure about that actually, Mr Brunton.

OMG. You were going to steal it?

Outrageous! I don't think you deserve much consideration!

What does it matter?! At least I have the satisfaction of knowing the truth! At least now I have the answers I was looking for! I've unravelled the secrets of the Musgrave Riddle that have plagued my family for so long! More importantly I have found the treasure!

I'm going to have to disappoint you there once again, Mr Brunton. I'm afraid your search for a Musgrave Treasure has been rather more wrapped up in the theatrical than the truth!

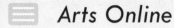

Arts Online

News > Theatre > London

THEATRICAL TREASURES UNCOVERE

Reginald Musgrave

Renovations to a top London school have resulted in an unexpected find of historical importance to the Arts community.

Baker Street Academy in west London was the scene of the incredible discovery, as a long-forgotten stash of theatrical stage props, costume jewellery and performance memorabilia was unearthed beneath the school's original wing.

The fantastic trove was the property of Reginald Musgrave, a once-famous Victorian theatre star who was the last private resident and owner of the building, which was then called Musgrave House.

The King Charles Players

As well as being a popular figure in his heyday, Musgrave was a founding member of an acting collective known as "The King Charles Players" who were regular performers at the London Victoria Theatre, which is still going strong today.

The Musgrave Treasure

The discovery brings to light a veritable wealth of

Victorian performance memorabilia, much of which had been forgotten in the 150-plus years since Reginald Musgrave passed away, leaving his grand house to an educational trust. Many of the exciting props and costume jewellery were from a popular play of time, based on the reign of King Charles I, called "The Musgrave Treasure", in which Reginald Musgrave was the star until the last performance in 1879.

Find of the Century

Current theatre director Howard Crawford has called it "the find of the century" and plans to bring several productions from the King Charles Players' era back to the London stage over the coming seasons. The Victoria theatre, along with the B&A museum, will jointly look after the newly discovered collection for future generations to enjoy.

Pictured: Baker Street Academy headmistress Mrs Cavendish

Baker Street Academy headteacher Mrs Cavendish said, "We are absolutely delighted with the extraordinary discovery and hope that it will only add to the outstanding reputation of the school."

One person who is particularly pleased with the find is school caretaker Mr Ralph Musgrave, who is

a distant relative of the Victorian thespian. "I'm over the moon about it," Mr Musgrave told our reporter. "I had always been told that there was a real connection to Baker Street Academy in our family, but we never knew much about it. To have it confirmed and find all of this fantastic history is just wonderful news! And to think it had been down there all that time! How exciting!"

Comments:

Ninjacatgurl: Woooooo! I always knew Baker Street Academy was special! I can't believe everyone thought it was a ghost, of course I wasn't scared...

Wow! That was a crazy few days. Even by Sherlock standards! Everything had happened in a blur since we discovered a secret cellar underneath Baker Street Academy and found our missing teacher Mr Brunton - along with the "Musgrave Treasure". Martha and I still had questions though, and as usual I suspected Sherlock would have answers...

So... Mr Brunton was using the Musgrave Riddle to try and discover hidden treasure at Baker Street Academy all along...

Yes.

Because his distant relative was the butler when Reginald Musgrave lived here and it was called Musgrave House...

Right again, John!

And it was this butler who originally tried to find a hidden treasure but mysteriously went missing?

Supposedly! The truth is that the butler of Musgrave House was never really missing. He was caught snooping and fired by Reginald Musgrave! It was newspaper reports that spread rumours of his disappearance.

So, just to check - that skeleton down in the cellar wasn't real then. You're sure about that, right?!

Haha! I couldn't be more certain, John. It was a theatrical prop!

And the 'Musgrave Treasure' was from a play, right? It wasn't really King Charles's royal treasure?

That's right, Martha. Not the sort of royal treasure that Mr Brunton had hoped for anyway! I said before that the Musgraves had an interesting history. When I was doing my research, I discovered that they actually did have connections to King Charles in the 17th century, before his untimely execution! It was around the same time that the family must have left Hurlstone. But there's no evidence of forgotten treasure! Even so, I imagine that distant connection must've been the inspiration behind the The Musgrave Treasure play, and the 'King Charles Players.'

Musgrave Treasure

So that's why the Musgrave Riddle mentions those things?

Exactly. I think the same thoughts became an obsession for Mr Brunton. After reading the Musgrave Riddle and discovering the family's royal connection, he must have become convinced with the idea that somehow, Musgrave House - or Baker Street Academy as we know it - was hiding some real **ROYAL TREASURE** left behind from King Charles I!

"Wow! No wonder he was trying to find it," I said.

"That would've been amazing if it was actually royal treasure though," mused Martha excitedly.

You can still call it amazing, Martha! What we discovered down in the cellar was more than just props and costume jewellery from a play. It was a lifetime's collection: Reginald Musgrave's very own theatrical legacy. And while it wasn't technically royal treasure, it was most certainly treasure in his eyes. Musgrave Treasure! And a Musgrave Mystery! And the **MUSGRAVE RIDDLE** had the answers all along if it could only have been understood properly.

So Mr Musgrave was sort of right when he said that the Musgrave Riddle was a game?

That about sums it up, John! In fact, the whole tangled mystery was just one big performance on the part of Reginald Musgrave. As a last act of theatrical flair, he hid his treasures and left the Riddle as the clue to find them! It was his way of keeping his legacy safe for a future generation. But after he died, the true meaning and relevance of the Musgrave Riddle was almost forgotten.

Until you and your super brain managed to work it out!

Musgrave Riddle

Precisely! It's a good thing that Baker Street Academy was here to keep Musgrave House alive and the secret of the Musgrave Riddle safe for all those years!

155

The Three Students

"Hey, speaking of the Riddle," I said, "what about the last lines?"

"Yeah!" echoed Martha. "When we were following it down to the secret cellar, we never got to the end. What about the curse? And the ghost? I mean, if Mr Brunton was only interested in finding the Musgrave Treasure ... who or what was behind all the spooky goings-on at school?!"

Sherlock looked at us mischievously. "Who do you think?"

"I don't know," I said. "That's why I asked you! Oh..." I felt a shiver as a thought occurred to me. "You mean there really is a ghost?" Martha's jaw dropped open and Sherlock's face lit up with a smile.

Don't be ridiculous, John! I've told you both already, there's no such thing as ghosts! Mr Brunton was the Baker Street Ghost! You remember my little demonstration with the lantern and the blazer?

Whoa! You mean to tell me he was behind all the other spookiness at Baker Street Academy too?

Precisely, John! Albeit with some 'assistance' from Charlie Milverton and Sebastian Moran.

Oh no! Mr Brunton had no idea what he was getting into with those two! I kinda feel sorry for him a bit now...

Not necessary, Martha. Mr Brunton was most definitely the architect of his own downfall! From that very first night when he appeared in his guise as the ghost, Mr Brunton had been trying to scare Mr Musgrave away from Baker Street Academy. Although I believe the first incident in the Old Library was somewhat fortunate...

When Mr Brunton saw how it affected the whole school, he was presented with a much easier opportunity to create confusion around the Old Wing of Baker Street Academy than he'd first imagined. And after finding two pupils who are no strangers to causing trouble anyway, he took full advantage of Charlie and Seb to ramp up the spookiness and spread rumours of ghosts, curses and hauntings through the classrooms.

That figures! No wonder they've been so annoying around school recently.

I've no doubt that they were behind the mysterious graffiti warnings appearing in school, as well as the classroom smoke incident! And of course, where Charlie Milverton and Sebastian Moran are concerned, it should be no surprise that there was not just a little bit of encouragement from our other favourite BSA student...

You mean, James Moriarty?! Ugh! I should've guessed.

Exactly, Martha. He's been getting regular updates from Charlie and Seb all along! I'm certain he found it an irresistible opportunity to cause some extra trouble for Baker Street Academy, Mr Brunton and us - from a safe distance!

That explains the annoying smarmy postcards he's been sending us!

Indeed. More than that though, he should never be underestimated.

As for the details with Mr Brunton, you know I was suspicious from the start where 'ghosts' were concerned. I started to investigate both the school and the Musgrave history for myself. My suspicions grew further when Mr Brunton so conveniently happened to bump into us that afternoon in the Old Library.

Because he was already snooping around trying to figure out where the clues in the Musgrave Riddle would lead him...

It was obvious to me that he'd already been searching for something, and when we found the section of the Musgrave Riddle that he dropped, I knew I was on to something.

"Once we realized Mr Brunton was missing, the whole picture started to appear. The riddle seemed to echo so much of what had been going on, it was clearly the key linking all of the strange events at Baker Street Academy."

"Wow! It's definitely been a tangled mystery," I said.

"Indeed it has, John!" said Sherlock with a very satisfied look on his face. "And that's exactly the way I like them!"

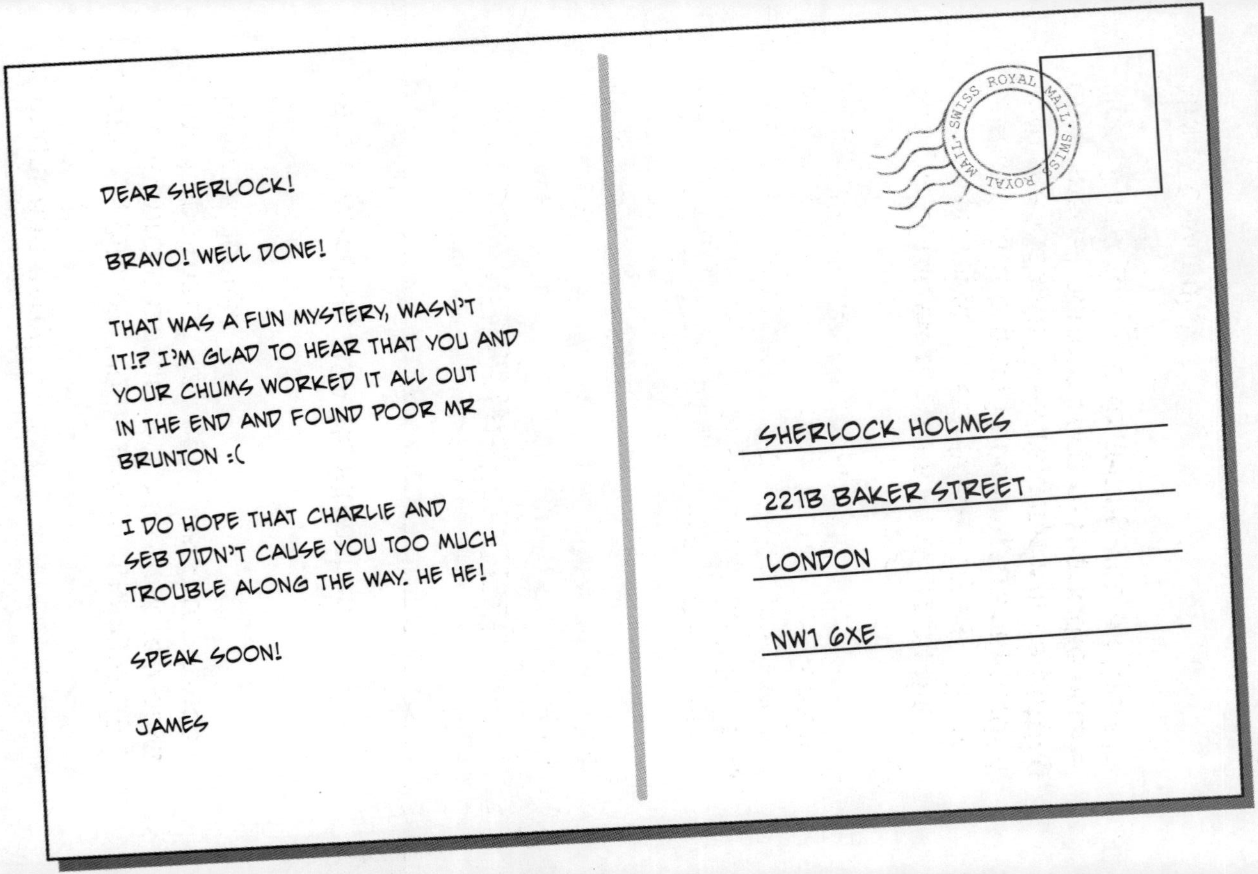

DEAR SHERLOCK!

BRAVO! WELL DONE!

THAT WAS A FUN MYSTERY, WASN'T
IT!? I'M GLAD TO HEAR THAT YOU AND
YOUR CHUMS WORKED IT ALL OUT
IN THE END AND FOUND POOR MR
BRUNTON :(

I DO HOPE THAT CHARLIE AND
SEB DIDN'T CAUSE YOU TOO MUCH
TROUBLE ALONG THE WAY. HE HE!

SPEAK SOON!

JAMES

SHERLOCK HOLMES

221B BAKER STREET

LONDON

NW1 6XE

ROYAL MAIL · SWISS ROYAL
MAIL · SWISS

160

bright and early!

Once again, we would like to apologize for the enforced closure over the last few days and hope that it has not caused too much inconvenience.

Mrs Cavendish, BSA Headteacher.

School Refurbishment!
Today 11:14

Dear BSA students,

I am delighted to announce that the refurbishment of the school's original building has now been completed. Very excitingly there will be a grand reopening as the new Baker Street Academy Arts Wing!

In light of the extraordinarily exciting discovery at Baker Street Academy, we will be celebrating the grand opening in conjunction with the Victoria Theatre, who will be putting on a special performance to mark the occasion. I look forward to seeing you all there!

Mrs M Cavendish

The Victoria Theatre proudly presents
the New King Charles Players in:

THE
MUSGRAVE
RIDDLE

Celebrating the Grand Opening of
the Baker Street Academy Arts Wing

THE
SHOW
MUST
GO ON!

After the dust had settled from the excitement
and craziness of the last few weeks at school,
things were finally getting back to normal.
Sherlock had been basking in the glow of a freshly
solved problem, and on top of a performance in
the newly opened Arts Wing, the extremely grateful
Victoria Theatre had given us *free* tickets to
see a play of our choosing! (Add that to the free
museum passes we got given from the B&A last
year, and maybe in future I shouldn't make such a
big deal out of all the trouble we've been mixed up
in since I've been at Baker Street Academy!)

221B felt a little quieter though, as Baskerville had gone back home to stay with Mr & Mrs Musgrave - but it did mean more lounging space and less going out for walkies! Martha and I decided we should make the most of a well-deserved quiet afternoon to relax, get comfy, and get reading in our favourite old armchairs... The peace and quiet didn't last too long though; it was almost impossible to ignore Sherlock as he dragged and clunked a *giant* trunk into the living-room, opened it up in the middle of the floor and started littering an assortment of objects all over the carpet around it...

I could recognize a few familiar items amongst the growing pile, like the old-fashioned lamp and shimmery blazer that Mr Brunton had used to pretend he was the Baker Street ghost, as well as a copy of the Musgrave Riddle.

"Sherlock! What are you doing?" I asked. "Aside from making a big mess..."

"Making a mess?" said Sherlock, pretending to sound offended. "I'm organizing the data, John! Seeing as you enjoy writing about our adventures so much, it seems only fair to keep a visual record too, don't you think?

"Jeez, Sherlock! Can't we just have a few days without having to think about adventure?!" pleaded Martha. "Ever since the Alpine Star business last

term, we can't seem to go five minutes round here without trouble sticking to us like poo on a shoe!

"Poo? On a shoe?" Sherlock and I burst out laughing.

"Yeah!" laughed Martha, joining in. Now she was really on a roll: "I blame you, Sherlock! All your 'data gathering, mystery chasing and problem solving' seems to do is attract even more problems!"

"Oh well, Martha," said Sherlock, smiling at me across the clutter. "The more the merrier, I say. There's nothing like a good mystery to solve and get the brain fired up, is there? Besides, it's not really my fault. None of the problematic stuff was happening before John came along!"

"Tut! John."

"Hey!"

Nice to see you all having so much fun!
I thought my three favourite detectives could do with a little treat!
Ooh, hot chocolate! Thanks Mrs Hudson!
You're welcome. But I do hope you're going to clean up all this mess?!
Busted! Ha ha!
Just cataloguing our adventures, Mrs Hudson. It's important business!
Oh yes, I'm sure it is. Jolly good!
I suppose it won't be long now before you're all off on your next adventure anyway!
MUUUUUUUM!

LolMail.

Hello Sweetie!

From: **Mummy**
To: **Watson, John**

Thursday 21st,

Hello John, sweetie,

I just wanted to send you a quick message before
you all go off on your super-exciting school trip. Mrs
Hudson has been in touch with all the details and
dates. It sounds like it's going to be a lot of fun going
skiing – how lucky you are! Your dad and I hope you
have a brilliant time with your friends. Be happy and
stay safe and try to send us a postcard!

Lots of love from Mum and Dad x x x x

END...

DEAR SHERLOCK,

GOOD NEWS!

IT LOOKS LIKE WE'LL BE SEEING EACH
OTHER SOON AFTER ALL! WHAT FUN - A
SCHOOL TRIP TO SWITZERLAND NO LESS!

AND TO THINK, I MIGHT EVEN BE ABLE
TO SHOW YOU AROUND SOME OF MY
FAVOURITE PLACES.

I KNOW - I CAN'T WAIT! SUCH A SHAME
YOU CAN'T BE HERE RIGHT NOW THOUGH.
I'M SURE YOU'RE ABSOLUTELY GOING TO
LOVE REICHENBACH IN THE FALL.

UNTIL THEN,

M X

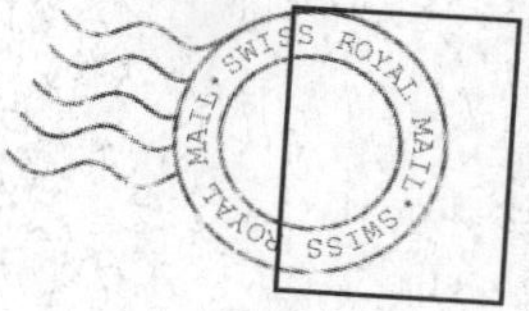

SHERLOCK HOLMES

221B BAKER STREET

LONDON

NW1 6XE

Acknowledgements

Huge thanks once again to: Sam, Liam, Andrew, Gen and everybody else working hard behind the scenes at team Scholastic U.K. to bring these books to life. It is much appreciated!

Thanks to Jeffrey West for his nice emails, Nancy Mercado, Nina Goffi, Baily Crawford and Melissa Schirmer and the rest of the team at Scholastic U.S for giving Sherlock a home across the pond too! And also to the many overseas publishers and teams who have published translations of Sherlock so far.

Thanks to Julie and the team at Lancashire schools library services, along with the wonderful primary schools and pupils involved with the Fantastic Book Awards.

And thanks to all my family and friends who've helped out whilst I've been working on Sherlock books, because I have probably been a nuisance! That includes special mentions for people like: Emily Lamm, Jamie at Elephant & Bird, Ian Cunliffe and Christian Mizon, and once again the lovely people at Artisan East Sheen along with the nice people I've met whilst frequenting the establishment!

Finally, thanks again to the Conan Doyle estate for the official stuff.

JUST WHO IS SAM HEARN?

OK, I've done a bit more digging since our last adventure and here's what I've been able to find about him so far:

He's been drawing and messing around in children's books for almost 20 years now... If that wasn't bad enough, it looks like he's started getting away with writing in them too! And he's definitely still been following us around here at Baker Street academy - I've found the evidence!

www.instagram.com/baker.street.academy/

See?! On top of all that, It also looks like he's recently been a Fantastic Book Award winner!

I'll let you know as a soon as I find out anything else.